This Walker book belongs to:

_____

_____

_____

First published 1988, 1994 and 2004 in *Out and About*,
Hiding and *Olly and Me* by Walker Books Ltd
87 Vauxhall Walk, London SE11 5HJ

This edition published 2016

2 4 6 8 10 9 7 5 3 1

© 1988, 2004 Shirley Hughes
Additional text © 2016 Shirley Hughes

This book has been typeset in Plantin Light Educational

Printed in China

British Library Cataloguing in Publication Data:
a catalogue record for this book is available from the British Library

ISBN 978-1-4063-7284-7

www.walker.co.uk

THE NURSERY COLLECTION

WINTER

Shirley Hughes

WALKER BOOKS
AND SUBSIDIARIES
LONDON • BOSTON • SYDNEY • AUCKLAND

Saturday Shopping

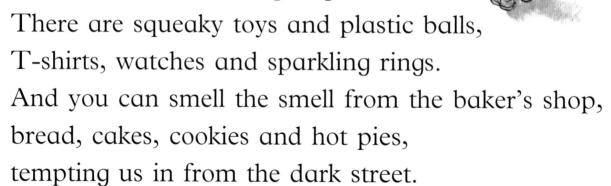

Saturday is a shopping day.
Olly and I don't like shops much,
but we like the market
when the stalls are all lit up,
and there are crowds of people.
I hold on tight to Dad's hand
while we load Olly's buggy
with apples, grapes and bananas
and sometimes even a pumpkin.
There are squeaky toys and plastic balls,
T-shirts, watches and sparkling rings.
And you can smell the smell from the baker's shop,
bread, cakes, cookies and hot pies,
tempting us in from the dark street.

Hoping

Grey day,
Dark at four,
Hurry home,
Shut the door.
Think of a time
When there will be
Decorations
On a tree,
Tangerines,
And hot mince pies,
A bulging stocking,
A Christmas surprise!

Cold

Cold fingers,
Cold toes,
Pink sky,
Pink nose.
Hard ground,
Bare trees,
Branches crack,
Puddles freeze,
Frost white,
Sun red,
Warm room,
Warm bed.

Ice in the Park

It's cold in the park, cold, cold,
And the wind blows sharp and keen.
The path's frosted over,
White as chalk.
Too cold to stand still,
Too cold to walk,
Better to run,
Better to shout,
Holler and wave your arms about,
See your breath come out like steam.

There's ice on the lake,
So the ducks can't swim;
Only one little hole for diving in.
It's cold in the park, cold, cold;
No more leaves on the tree.
It's almost too cold for the hungry birds,
And too cold for Olly and me.

Sick

Hot, cross, aching head,

Prickly, tickly, itchy bed.

Piles of books and toys and puzzles

Heavy on my feet,

Pillows thrown all anyhow,

Wrinkles in the sheet.

Sick of medicine, lemonade,

Soup spooned from a cup.

When will I be *better*?

When can I *get up*?

Three in a Bed
Three in a bed
Under the cover,
Bemily, me
And Olly my brother.
He's at one end,
We're at the other,
Warm in bed
Under the cover.

Flowers need to hide in the ground
in wintertime.

But they come peeping out again
in the spring.